The Short End of Madness
By Heidi Hess

For all things Heidi Hess follow her on social media:

Facebook: @Heidi A Hess
Facebook: @heidicreates01
Facebook: @ReadItWriteItBookFestival

Instagram: createsheidi
Instagram: readitwriteitbookfestival

Twitter: @createsheidi
Twitter: @readitwriteitfl

Or visit her website: heidicreates.net

Also by Heidi Hess

Fiction

Chasing Elpis, included in the anthology *A Light That Never Goes Out* published by Neon Sunrise Publishing.

Longing, included in the anthology *LOVE//LOST* published by Neon Sunrise Publishing.

Higher Signal, included in the anthology *Dead Signals//Lost Transmissions* published by Neon Sunrise Publishing.

Spin The Bottle, included in the anthology *It's All Fun And Games Until Somebody Dies* published by D&T Publishing.

Non-Fiction

Mom Moments bi-monthly in <u>aroundwellington.com</u>

The Short End of Madness
Copyright © 2022 by Heidi Hess

www.heidicreates.net

Cover art is by Heidi Creates

Published in the United States in 2022 with KDP

ISBN:

Dedicated to the Sun, the Stars, and the Moon

Special thanks to the second half of the sisters, Polaris, the Jinks, The Tribe, and Copperpoint.

For these people, I am eternally grateful.

The Short End Of Madness

By Heidi Hess

No great mind has ever existed
                without a touch of madness.
                                - Aristotle

Table of Contents

Woad is the Way

The liquid on the brush was dripping off the end and creating
puddles all over the sink and countertop. Jane couldn't have
cared less about the mess it created. What was important was
that she readied herself for the next step. The fluorescent light
bulb in her bathroom flickered and blinked, almost trying to
flash a warning… You've gone too far this time. What will
they think? She shoved that voice out of her mind and
embraced her newfound purpose, her newfound confidence.
She stared at her reflection in the generic medicine cabinet
mirror. This was someone she didn't recognize, but she felt that
this was the person she was always meant to be… blue eyes,

blue hair, and now for the final piece. She raised the brush to her face and painted a long vertical indigo stripe that began at her forehead, down her nose, and over her chin. Yes, this felt right. Now to complete her transformation. Jane was gone. This was Raine. And she was ready.

————

Las Vegas was an interesting place to be a psychologist. It seemed everyone here had some kind of problem. Jane had only started her practice here two years ago, but she had more than a few regular patients and they all seemed to respond to her specialty—color theory therapy. She was able to take people to their most painful memories, and with the use of color help them deal with their emotions and the pain attached to those memories. She loved what she was doing and couldn't have been happier professionally. Personally was a different story. After leaving the small town of Rachel, NV to pursue her education, she had difficulty connecting with people. Everyone was so different outside of the little town she had grown up in. But she tried and kept trying… she had a few girlfriends but no boyfriend. This distressed her parents greatly. They had pushed for her to fit in, to be popular, to be just like all the other girls her age, and she certainly did try but something had always been off.

Jane considered all of these things driving home, letting the Vegas neon consume her sight. *Lord,* she thought, *someone really ought to study the effect the neon color has on a person's psyche.* It was blinding. She turned her thoughts to the evening ahead of her. Her parents, Clark and Coraline, were in town and she was expecting them for dinner. Sigh… there would be questions… how are things? Why don't you have a boyfriend? Why aren't you married? Ugh. Was it too late to call a male escort to pretend to be her beau just to get them off her back? She chuckled at the thought and threw it aside.

Her parents arrived on time. She hugged and kissed them as warmly as she could and led them to the dining room for dinner. There was a definite change in tone compared to the last time she saw them. Her mother wouldn't meet her gaze, and her father was tight and serious. Jane poured herself a glass of white wine and was in the process of pouring her mom a glass when she decided to get right to it. "It's great to see you," she lied, "but what's going on? You both seem on edge." Her mother looked at her father and grabbed his hand. "What's going on?" Jane pressed. Her father broke the silence. "Jane, we have to tell you something. It's important that you know." Jane finished pouring her dad his wine and sat down in her chair, bracing herself for what was next.

Her dad looked at her and put his rough hand on her arm. His slender face was unusually pale and he was beginning to sweat. His glasses slid down his nose, so he pushed them up and adjusted himself in his seat. He was now sitting up straight and tall. He took a deep breath and began. "What do you remember about living in Rachel?" he inquired. Jane thought for a second. She remembered everything. Rachel was where she grew up, where she had spent her childhood, and she had only good memories of that small town. "What do I remember?" she repeated. "Uh, everything. I remember playing in the yard with Teela and making mud pies. I remember sitting on the porch coloring with Mom." Her mother interrupted, "Darling, there's a reporter who has been interviewing people. He's doing an exclusive story on the children of Rachel. He may contact you." Jane shook her head, grimaced a little, and took a sip of wine. "Mom, why would they want to talk to me?" Her parents shared a look. "Jane," her dad interjected, "what I am about to tell you will seem unbelievable. And looking back now, I know we did the wrong thing. But it was, well, we thought it was for science." He grabbed his wife's hand and looked at her. "It was all for science."

Over the next two hours, Jane sat and listened to her parents remind her of their proximity to Area 51 and how the military had a constant presence in the town. Her dad worked at a classified lab run by the military, which Jane knew but they didn't talk about it. "You were about three years old so, of course, you don't remember this," Mom continued, "but we were approached to participate in a study. The military had a program to test the effects of certain brain games on kids. They needed people committed to science and also people they could trust. These games were developed by the extraterrestrials living in Area 51. You were one of several kids selected to participate. They told us that it had the potential to increase your brain function by double." Her mom finished but she just stared down at the table. Jane sat with her mouth agape. She closed her eyes and wracked her brain, searching for a distant memory. She remembered a night when she was very little… a bright blue light right outside her window. It didn't frighten her and she didn't feel the need to tell her parents. She remembered feeling happy seeing this light… and whatever it was that was creating it. "Jane, they would come to get you at night," her dad said carefully, "so it would seem like you were—" Jane cut him off, "Like I was dreaming. I remember. A blue light would fill my room, but that's all I remember."

They sat in silence for what seemed like an eternity. Then her parents looked at one another and reached out to her, putting a hand on her arm and back. All Jane could do was look at the floor. It was then that she realized what her parents had done… had let aliens do to her. Jesus. The tears came and they wouldn't stop. She continued to stare at the floor while she uttered, "I was little… I…I trusted you… and you… you let them take me?" Blinded by her tears she glanced up at them. "How could you?" Her mom was the first to speak. "Jane, it was for science." Her voice was heavy with emotion as she fought back tears. "We shouldn't have done it, but what's done is done."

Jane stood up. "What's done is done?" she repeated. "I think you should leave." She moved to the door and opened it. Her parents protested but eventually, they left. Jane dried her tears. She was numb and tired, and sat down in front of the TV. She had turned it on but it was just a blank blue screen. She stared at it for the next few hours, not realizing that there was nothing on the screen. It made her feel comforted… like everything was going to be okay. She finally fell into a deep sleep—the kind you experience as a child. And while she slept she got a powerful message. One she couldn't ignore.

The next morning she set about making the necessary changes. She got ready for her day and as she picked out her jeans, navy shirt, and navy blazer she felt a surge of energy pulsing through her. Breakfast consisted of blueberries, and she devoured them as she called her patients to explain that for the unforeseeable future she would not be able to assist them on their mental health journey, and that she wished them the best. For a second she heard her old familiar inner voice speaking.

What are you doing?? She ignored it, filling up a garbage bag with clothes and things that weren't blue. A new voice spoke now—*The only things that are real, the only things you can trust now, are blue. Everything else must go.* She had created quite a pile at the end of the driveway. She looked around at the landscaping around her house. It was funny how she had subconsciously picked only blue flowers. There was a vacant field next to her house. It was a radiant shimmering gold in the Nevada sunshine, and for some reason it was fine with her. She decided to take a walk among the small yellow wildflowers. When she returned she called her folks to ask for their help. There were still a few things that needed to be taken care of and, after all, what's done is done.

Clark and Coraline's car stopped at the end of the driveway. They peered out at the huge pile of miscellaneous things… her table, chairs, bags upon bags of garbage. Their faces when Jane answered the door were ones of confusion. "Jane, what's happening here?" her mom inquired. She looked at Jane and peered around her and saw that, just like her clothes and makeup, everything in the house was blue. "Nothing, Mom. I've never felt better. Come with me. I want to show you something."

After her stroll the other day in the field adjacent to her house, she was filled with peace. She went back home, researched what it could be, and realized that the entire field was a plant called Woad. It has been used for centuries to dye things blue. She picked a bunch of the leaves and ground them up… it turned out the sap was a blue liquid that could dye things. She marveled at her luck in ending up with a field of plants next to her house that dyed things blue. She had to show her parents; surely they would marvel at this as well and appreciate the irony.

"Jane," her dad barked. "Where the hell are we going? It's getting dark." Her mom chimed in as well, "If I had known we'd be out here I would have worn my sneakers. My heels are sinking into the ground." Jane glanced back at them. She led them to a large circular opening in the field. The sky was growing dark and the stars were just visible. "I don't know why you brought us out here, but this is ridiculous!" Her father was angry at having been brought out here. Her mother tried to touch her. "Jane, it's getting dark. And frankly, your behavior is scaring me." The inner voice spoke to her again: *Just do what you have to do… they don't appreciate the Woad… do what you have to do…* Jane looked out at the field and sighed. "My name isn't Jane anymore. From now on I will be known as Raine. It is the name they have chosen for me."

From her navy blazer she pulled out an envelope. The blue ink read, "To Coraline and Clark." She handed it to her parents. "Here, this is for you. Read it later. I need you to take the things at the end of the driveway and donate them." Her parents stared at her. They didn't have enough time to say anything before they saw the gun in her hand. "Now, go…" They both gasped. Raine continued, "What's done is done, right?" She aimed her gun at them. Their eyes were blank pieces of glass reflecting the blue night sky with so many unanswered questions. *One day they would appreciate the Woad.* They backed away slowly, carefully. Raine watched them until they were little specks of dark blue in the distance.

———

It was almost time now. She stared at her reflection in the mirror. The indigo stripe down her face was beautiful. They would love it. They would appreciate it. She dipped her brush again and again, painting her entire body. When the dyeing was complete, she admired her new blue skin and walked out into the field. She was surrounded by the Woad and she could feel the energy of the blue, radiant all around her. She was ready. She closed her eyes, and before she could even think it again that familiar bright blue light came down from the sky. She lifted her chin, stretched her arms out to her sides, opened herself up to it, and allowed it to fill her. She was going home. She was really going home.

A Safe Distance

Andy Bransen's long legs buckled underneath him. He fell into the dirt face-first, completely exhausted. He had been defeated yet again. This wasn't his first time running away. No, he had only been thirteen years old on his first attempt. Even at the tender age of thirteen, he knew that things at home weren't right and that they were just going to get worse. After his dad died, his mother moved on rather quickly. Living on a large farm in Kansas in 1920 meant that you needed lots of strong people to make it work. Andy, being eleven at the time, had tried to help his mom but it wasn't enough. So, when his mom went out and brought home a "friend", he was happy to have another man in the house. For his sake, and hers. Ivan was a burly overgrown man ten years her senior. He was loud and boisterous. In the beginning, he laughed easily and played catch with Andy. Eventually, his mom married him. Looking back on it, that's really when the trouble started.

Darkened woods surrounded Andy. Sitting up, he brushed the hair and dirt from his face and found a rock to lean up against. He stared at the night sky and thought about his dad and what life would have been like if he had survived the accident. Things would have been so different. Instead of waking up to yelling, he would have listened to the radio and gone to sleep softly. His bedroom door never would have been thrown open in the middle of the night, and he never would have known what whisky smelled like on a grown man's breath. At school, bruises never would have had to be explained and he wouldn't have become good at mending torn pajamas. Life would have been different.

Attempt number one took him to the highway. Shelby was a small town, so when Andy ran away and was caught by the police they brought him right back home and he paid for it. After that incident, things went south at school. The phone call from Mrs. Williams came in after one particular episode involving a boy named Tim. "Mom, you don't understand," Andy insisted. "Young man, this wasn't just a fistfight. He passed out from being hit so hard and they had to pull you off of him? You just can't do things like this when you get angry," his mom said as she crossed her arms and looked at him from across the table. She continued. Her voice was softer now. "They're recommending we get you some help. Mrs. Williams mentioned the pictures you've drawn and said that there might be something wrong." Andy can still see her eyes filling up with tears. "Mom. I'm fine." Andy couldn't bring himself to tell her that he was anything but fine. He decided that he would take care of it himself. He was still young but he knew that he had to remove himself, and if he couldn't do it physically then he would do it with his mind.

The nightly visits continued, but Andy got smart. He made sure that his mom made the weekly trip to the liquor store to get Ivan enough whiskey to ensure him passing out or being very clumsy. Andy moved his bed near the window and would sleep with it open. If Ivan came crashing into his bedroom in his clumsy drunken stupor, all he had to do was jump out the window. This strategy frequently worked, but not all the time. And it was during those times that things got progressively violent.

That was where Andy was now. Fifteen years old, cold, dirty, leaned up against a rock and grateful for the peace. He couldn't take it anymore. The medicine that they prescribed him was making him slow and less likely to escape Ivan. Andy pretended to take it to make his mom happy.

This was his second attempt. He made it past town and into the woods along the highway. He planned to keep running until he couldn't run anymore. He had to get as far away as he could —farther than the last time. The night noises surrounded him and you would think that Andy would have been scared. But which is worse—the hell you know or the hell you don't know? He decided that whatever was out there was worth the gamble. And so, leaning against the rock and clutching a bag he had packed, he closed his eyes and fell asleep.

Andy was startled awake by the sound of branches being broken and loud voices. The bright lights shone directly in his eyes and he was stunned. "Well, there you are. We've been out all night looking for you!" Sheriff Hillard exclaimed. Andy was shocked. How did he find him? He scrambled to his feet. His first and only thought was, "No… I can*not* go back." He launched himself around the rock, unsure of his surroundings, and ran right into the volunteers who were out helping to look for him. They reached out to console him but he thrashed and bucked, trying desperately to get away. His struggle was futile. They led him to the cruiser and put him in the backseat. The tears came and he didn't fight it. The voice was speaking again. At first softly: *Would he ever be able to escape? Was there no release? NO MERCY?*

The lights were on when they pulled into the driveway. There was a large van in the driveway, one he had never seen before. His mind raced. On the drive home, he had pushed past the sadness and allowed his circumstances to dictate his next moves. He felt like a caged animal—fierce and ready to spring. Ivan was waiting for him on the porch. Behind him stood his mother in the screened doorway. Light spilled out around Ivan's large frame, leaving a menacing shadow on the landing. The sheriff got out of the cruiser and opened Andy's door. At first his steps were light, and then they increased in speed and there was a scream that came from him as he attacked Ivan on the steps. He may have been a scrawny fifteen-year-old kid, but he was strong. Sure enough Ivan went down hard, hitting his head on the deck. And before he knew it, Andy was pummeling him with everything he had. The voice, in between laughing, was urging him on: "Hit it! Hit him hard! Keep him down!" All that drunk Ivan could do was hold his arms up against such a fierce attack. Over the commotion and obscenities being muttered he heard her voice. It was his mom. "STOP IT, ANDY! STOP IT RIGHT NOW!" The sheriff was trying to pull him off and his mom was by his side, but there was someone else. A tall, slender man with a calm disposition. "Hold him still," he said. Andy's eyes turned to his mom to question who this was, but before he could ask he was thrown down on the porch at the same level as Ivan. He got a glance at his handiwork. Ivan's face was a bloody, bruised mess but his eyes said it all. There was a smile there… a cunning smile that told Andy that he had the upper hand. Ivan stood. "See? I told you he was crazy," he gloated. His mom was now crying into her hands. The stranger put a hand on her back and stated, "We can help him." The last thing Andy remembered was a sharp pain in his arm, feeling drowsy, and being put into the back of the strange van.

When Andy came to he thought he was in heaven. Everything was white. The walls were white and lined with something unfamiliar—were those pillows? He lifted his head. It was the only part of his body that he *could* lift. He glanced down at his arms and legs. He had been tied down to a bed of some sort, and was no longer wearing his street clothes but a thin white nightgown. There was a door in front of him just past the foot of his bed with a small window. Beyond that he could hear voices, moans, and occasionally screaming. He was in the middle of deciphering where he was exactly when the door opened and that tall slender man walked in with a pretty blonde girl next to him. "Ahh… I see you're awake. Welcome, Andy. My name is Dr. Anton," he said, matter-of-factly. Andy remembered him and a look of disgust washed over his face. "I remember you. Where am I?" Andy said impatiently "And this?" He pulled against the restraints. "This is very uncomfortable." Dr. Anton spoke, "You have some violent tendencies. I can't take that chance, unfortunately, but not to worry. We will have you fixed in no time." Fixed? What did they need to fix? "Doctor, what do you mean 'fixed'?" Andy inquired. Over the next ten minutes, the doctor explained what they would be performing tomorrow morning. It was the latest in the treatment of the sickness. This would make his violent urges and the voice go away. It would make most thoughts go away. The woman next to him, Nurse Ann, shifted uneasily. She looked at them nervously from one to the other but never said a word. "This is something your parents have agreed on," the doctor stated. Andy's head was swimming. This couldn't be, but what choice did he have? He could try and run away again, but to what end? This was it. This was the end of the road and he knew, based on what the doctor had said, the way the nurse looked nervously at him, that he would end up with no thoughts at all. The doctor and nurse left. He rested his head on the pillow, staring up at the ceiling. Tears streamed down his face as he thought about his life and how unfair it had been. He wished he had been given another chance somewhere far away.

He must have fallen asleep, because when he awoke the overhead light was off. There was a little light coming in from the window and the nurse that had been in the room before was there with another girl. They made the SHHH sign and untied him. He sat up confused and looked at them. Ann spoke first. "I saw your chart. I know what happened to you because it happened to my sister," she whispered. "How could you possibly know?" Andy said. She glanced at him sideways. "So, how drunk did your stepdad have to get before he stopped hurting you?" She did know. Andy felt as if he had been found out, and at the same time a huge weight had been lifted off of his shoulders. Finally, someone understood. She continued. "Listen, I've seen what they do… You need to get out of here," she whispered, glancing around.

He dressed in his street clothes, but they wrapped him up in the sheets off of his bed. He climbed into the large bin that held the laundry. The girls wheeled the bin down a hall and outside. Ann was speaking again: "Andy, in about ten minutes a train stops in town and there are always open cars. Make sure you are on it. Take care of yourself…" He whispered his thanks, wiping tears away as he said it. He would never forget their kindness. He sat there and listened. Was that a door that opened? Where was the train? It seemed like forever but there… in the distance… a faint chugging sound… the huffing and puffing that only comes from a locomotive. It progressively got louder and slowed down, and when he couldn't stand it another minute he jumped out of the bin, shedding the white sheets and the shame that came along with his abuse. Here was his chance. His ticket out. And just as he had run so far and so long on that second failed attempt at running away, he was now doing the same thing. Only this time his legs wouldn't fail him the way society had failed him. He was taking his chance and jumped into an open car. He landed hard inside, rolled over, and looked up at the ceiling of the train car. He sat up and watched this strange town disappear. He had tried so hard to distance himself physically and mentally in the past… and now he would truly be distanced and absolutely free. And that felt pretty good.

Just Another Night

The train whistle heard in the distance was a signal that people, usually strangers, would be entering the bar relatively soon. Jenny wiped the bar down again. It was a nervous twitch for someone who had always been a bartender. She did this, she told herself, so things would be clean. But she also knew that it was a self-soothing hypnotic reflex.

Her final wipe with the bar towel was greeted with the front door opening, and in blew an attractive couple. They were arm in arm, their bodies slightly touching in several spots. The green neon on the wall reflected off his glasses as he approached and ordered two beers. The woman beside him, maybe half his size in height and stature, glanced at Jenny. She smiled a pleasant neon-green-tinged smile that told Jenny for her to leave them alone. She did just that.

The twosome sat at a darkened corner table. Her regulars were there and she found that comforting. She poured one of them another round and then started washing a few glasses. It kept her busy. She glanced up at the couple every few minutes. She couldn't help herself. They were now curled up into each other, whispering in each other's ear, giving little kisses. As far as they were concerned there was no one else in the bar. They were so close it was hard to differentiate one from the other in the dim light.

Jenny was just getting comfortable with them sitting there pawing at each other, when she heard odd sounds. It was more than groaning, and she was just getting ready to tell them to behave or get a room when she heard a *ripppp* followed by a gurgle. It was dark, but she could distinctly see something spilling on the floor. She sighed…another bunch of drunks to clean up after. Great. She grabbed her towel and walked over. The puddle was pooling out beyond the little table that sat between her and them. The smell of hot iron filled the air, and before she could put words to what that smelled like, the woman, who Jenny thought was sitting on the man's lap, turned to face her. Jenny gasped and stepped back. The woman's mouth was full of blood and a large hole had been torn open in the man's chest. Jenny continued to step back, her steps sounding wet from all the blood on the floor. She was nearly at the bar when the woman, mouth glistening, bared her fangs at Jenny and turned her full attention to the rest of the room. They didn't realize what was happening until the woman leaped from her spot in the corner to the bar top. There were audible gasps followed by a swift evacuation. The thing on the bar watched them leave, and that gave Jenny just enough time. She grabbed the shotgun and fired both rounds into this blood-starved fiend. It fell back onto the floor, a large gaping hole where an abdomen used to be. The thing turned over and was trying to claw its way out the door when Jenny grabbed the emergency stake. She launched herself over the bar, and in one motion turned over the demon and shoved the wooden stake deep into its heart.

The struggling stopped, its eyes glazed over, and its head fell to the side. Jenny sat back on her heels and wiped her blood-splattered face with her sleeve. Nights like this were always difficult. She would have to replace the emergency wooden stake yet again, and the clean-up always took forever. She should really ask for a raise.

Desirable Delusions

Chapter 1

The wheel on the bright red shopping cart was rattling uncontrollably. It was just one more noise. The last straw on the audible haystack that was her life at that particular moment. The twins were in the cart. Collin was jumping up and down demanding for her to open his juice box: "JUIIICCEE" Camille, being the independent girl that she was at the tender age of two, was jamming the straw into the box, missing the hole and bending the straw. Camille sat in the cart, trying to avoid being stepped on by her jumping brother, looked at the straw, and burst into tears. Sabine had had it. She could feel the numbness setting in. She embraced it. It was safer this way. She fought back her own sobs and outburst by grabbing Collin's juice box with one hand and stabbing the straw into it with unnecessary force. Then Camille's. Apple juice spurted out onto her hand, but she didn't care. Her hair had fallen into her face and she pushed it back unconsciously with her juice-covered hand, slightly shaking as she handed the open container to be drained to her tear-stained daughter.

The cart was on automatic pilot now. They had their routine. Juice boxes, then books, then toys. The kids had calmed down. Apple juice was now their drug of choice, and these two were slipping into that heroine-like comatose state that signaled satiability. Sabine grabbed the kids their favorite board books —*Fancy Nancy* and *Bob the Builder*. Their stubby little juice-covered fingers flipped through the pages, pointing at this and that. Colors were what they were identifying right now. Sabine looked at Camille's *Fancy Nancy* book. The pictures of that little girl prancing around in her mom's high heels, sunglasses, and feather boas made Sabine think about her previous life. Camille turned the page. In the next shot Nancy had on a large red headdress complete with sparkly rhinestones. Camille pointed to it. "Red," she said. Sabine smiled, thinking of her old life. This was almost a replica of the headdress that she had worn. "Yes, red." She entertained the other parts of the costume and how it would look on her new body. None of these things were comfortable, but they had made her feel… well different than she did now. "Mom," Collin called her "Bob, ello…" She replied, "Yes, Collin. Good job. Bob's hat is yyyeeelllloooww." She over-pronounced the word, hoping that Collin would notice and pick up on how to say it properly. Yellow. Her mind wandered a bit. It was the color of his hair. That man she'd left so many years ago. She had traded him in for stability and the possibility of a family. And where did it get her? Her thoughts trailed off as she thought of him. What if she had stayed? And that's when it caught her eye.

A book. Its cover shined and sparkled almost like it was in the sun. It was at the end of the row of kids' books. What was it doing here? The cover was brightly hued and, ironically, had the suggested figure of a showgirl. There, emblazoned at the top of the cover, was the title—*Desirable Delusions*. She paused for a second before picking it up. How odd. It was of average weight and height. There didn't appear to be anything special about this book. Based on the title it was probably a murder mystery set in Vegas. A piece of paper stuck out of the top of the book. She opened the book to the page that had the paper. It read:

Dear Reader,

You need this book. It's my favorite for obvious reasons.

Enjoy,

A Store Associate.

The kids sat transfixed by their respective books, and now she was transfixed on something other than them. And the idea that the universe had picked a book out for her seemed impossible, but yet… here it was. She decided that everyone was getting their books today. Including her, grocery budget be damned. The rest of the trip was uneventful but there was a thread of something positive inside of her that was keeping her holding on. What could this book be about? And what did the random store associate mean by "It's my favorite for obvious reasons"?

The house was silent when Sabine finally got around to picking up the book. She curled up on the couch, a blanket draped over her legs, and held it in her hand for what seemed an eternity. The newness of the book made it stiff, but with a little effort she opened to page one and jumped in. She had been right. This book was about a showgirl, but there wasn't anything murder mystery about it. In fact, in some ways the book mirrored her old life with a few wonderful exceptions. Is this how life would have turned out? That was her last thought as she fell asleep. There was a period of peaceful darkness, and then when she woke she was on someone else's couch, in someone else's home. Her eyes darted about, looking for clues as to where she was… but she didn't have a clue.

"Sabine!" Someone was calling her name from the room beyond. "Sabine, you have to get up or—" She recognized that voice; it was Ted. "…come on lazy bones. Get up or you'll be late." He walked into the room, his signature blond locks just a little on the messy side and longer than they should be. He glided over to her and touched her arm gently. Sabine smiled in response to seeing him. She didn't say anything at first, she just took him all in. The gray shorts hung on his hips just so, and he always smelled of pine. God, it was good to see him again. She rose, and upon standing she realized that her body was not the one she knew… she was leaner, muscular. Ted pulled her to him. "You really need to go…" he whispered in her ear. She leaned into his embrace and curled her arms around his neck, gently weaving her fingers in his hair. Their faces were so close. The warmth of his breath was enticing but it was his deceptive lips that were the clincher… they were thin-looking but upon further inspection one found that they were plump, juicy, and generous. She leaned in and brushed her lips on his. "Hey now… we can't start this. You have a show." She stepped back and sighed. "I'll just stay here." She was joking, of course. "Now listen here, missy, you have worked your butt off to get into the Fire and Ice show and I won't let you waste that."

There was another period of darkness, and then she was being dropped off at the theater's backstage door. She walked in and was greeted by questions from a host of different people. She tried to answer them as best she could as she was ushered to the dressing room. It was a frantic race to get into her costume, do her makeup, and—wait! What was she supposed to do? She didn't know where to go or what to do. She gazed at her reflection in the mirror. It was her, but she was so different.

She inhaled sharply to calm her nerves. She would know what to do when she got out there.

Lights came up on the stage; a wall of fake flames were her backdrop as she danced to the beat of the music. Her headdress swayed and trailed behind her, making it look like there was a trail of flames devouring the stage as she danced. Every eye was on her and by the time she was done they were all on their feet, applauding and cheering for more. She breathed it all in. This moment was hers and she had never been happier. That night she lay in bed wrapped in Ted's arms, thoroughly exhausted from the performance and their feverish lovemaking. She considered her kids. Her home. Her husband. How long would this last? That was her last thought as the dark void took over again.

"MOMMYYYY!!!" The yelling pulled her back to reality. It was Collin. She bolted into the kitchen. There he was, standing in front of the fridge, getting ready to throw a fit if he didn't get his cereal. Camille was way ahead of him. The fridge opened, the Cocoa Corn Puffs box on the floor, lying on its side, spilled milk underneath this mess, and Camille was seated with a bowl of cereal placed in between her legs, using her fingers to eat. She was on her hands and knees, cleaning things up and trying to calm Collin, when Dan came in. He stepped over her and ignored the kids like he usually did to get his coffee "Gotta go! Can't be late." And with that he was out the door. He barely acknowledged her. She stopped cleaning for a second and sat back on her heels. She had been this thing of beauty in her dream and now… the continued thought just depressed her even further. Grabbing the Cocoa Corn Puffs box, she sat on the floor and leaned up against the cabinets. Camille continued to eat and Collin was still yelling. She took a hand full of cereal and popped it into her mouth. Her crunching was loud, but Collin's screaming was louder. "COLLIN! FOR THE LOVE OF GOD SHUT UP ALREADY!" she bellowed, spraying chewed-up bits of cereal on the floor, on both kids. Collin stopped screaming. He was shocked and scared, but he stopped yelling. She had never yelled at him with such ferocity, and she felt bad about it. But at the same time it had felt good to unleash herself. And then suddenly her mind shifted to the book. She wished she had the time to read it right now.

Chapter 2

Water was dripping off her hair and onto the beige carpet. Sabine was standing naked in front of her closet, looking for… something, but she wasn't sure what. The kids were wandering around outside her bedroom. Every now and then she could hear crunchy little steps on the kitchen floor turning the Cocoa Corn Puffs that were left from breakfast into Cocoa Corn dust. It registered with her, and at the same time she didn't care. She rifled through her clothes… no, no, no… they were all so boring. And then there, towards the back, was a red t-shirt. She ripped it off the hanger and threw it on. No sneakers today. She selected red kitten heels—where had they come from? She must have bought them years ago. It was Wednesday and today was lunch with the moms. Elise, Carrie, and Tanya would be there with their kids in tow at Chick-R-Us. They met there for camaraderie, good food, and a play area where they could just let the kids run free while they chatted. And on most days her twins would go in, there would be a scuffle, and they would leave tired from all the playing and Sabine happy for the common company.

Today had a different vibe. After the kids ate and ran off into the play area the moms commented on how vibrant she looked. They cooed over her heels, asking how one runs after a toddler in heels. There was a long pause… the moms weren't expecting a response but, as cool as a cucumber, she replied, "You don't." The ladies all exchanged glances and Carrie was the first to inquire, "Sabine, sweetie, is everything okay?" Another long awkward silence followed and then Sabine finally said, "Yes, Carrie. Everything is adequate." Sabine mulled over her response. Adequate? Where did that come from? It felt as if she were watching and hearing herself do and say things that weren't things she would normally do or say. And at the same time the conversation with her lady friends, which usually comforted her, seemed dull, drab… beige.

They left Chick-R-Us as usual, the twins screaming and crying from being exhausted. The numbness took over again but it was stronger now. She drove home and put them in their cribs and asked the neighbor to keep an eye on them so she could run out. Her car turned into the shopping center. She hadn't remembered driving here but here she was. Her eyes scanned the storefronts: Quik Mart, Nails by T, Insurance… and there on the end was a costume store. They would have what she needed. She parked and quickly headed into Minerva's Costume Shop.

Typical of smaller stores, there was a wind chime on the door that informed the merchant of a customer's presence. Sabine stepped in and scanned the small, dingy store. Row after row of costumes of every color of the rainbow could be found here. What was she looking for? She started down one row and was greeted by a short stout lady with large coke-bottle glasses. She waddled toward her. "Hello, dear… are you looking for something in particular ?" Sabine could feel her eyes glaze over as she explained to Minerva exactly what she was looking for.

She paid for the costume using the money set aside for the mortgage and then made a quick stop at the home improvement store and the gas station.

When she arrived home she thanked the neighbor and dismissed her. She had work to do. But first, while the kids were still taking their naps, she sat and opened the book. She started reading again and then that familiar darkness set in… but this time she knew where she was. She was in the show producer's office, holding a newspaper with a glowing review of her performance while she filled in for the older lead dancer. The review gushed: "She is the most radiant thing to hit the strip since the sun. We implore the management to make her a permanent fixture as the lead." The review was talking about her, and the producers and managers had brought her in to offer her the lead. She was thrilled! This was her dream. Another bout of darkness blanketed her and now she was in Ted's apartment and they were talking about their future together. Everything in the world was right. Everything was coming together.

And it was interrupted by loud crying. Instantly she was transported back to reality. It was Collin waking up from his nap. He would need to be changed. Both kids would need to be changed. Changed. That word sat with her. Changed… change… hum… she thought on it some more as she pulled Collin from his crib. His strong little legs kicked and squirmed. She grabbed a new diaper and Collin rolled over and was trying to get away. Sabine grabbed his ankle and pulled him back, and with his other leg he kicked as hard as he could in her stomach. He laughed a little. He thought it was funny. Sabine had the wind knocked out of her and when she recovered she had pulled Collin straight up in the air… holding him upside down by the ankle. She hadn't realized that she did this and gently set him down. And just like this morning, he had that same scared shocked look on his face. She changed his diaper (changed… change… there was that word again…) and set him on the floor. He scuttled off to play. Change. Yes, it was time for her to change. Camille whined and Sabine picked her up and set her on the floor as well. And then it was time for Sabine to change. She grabbed the book and headed to her closet. Where was that costume?

Chapter 3

Dan pulled into the driveway and sat in the car for a few moments. He looked at the house. The lights were on and he thought he smelled dinner cooking. Could that be pot roast? He breathed in the night air and relaxed at the thought of being home. He took the steps two at a time and grabbed the doorknob and opened the door. The kitchen floor was covered in milk and old cereal, and there was some odd music being played very loud. Collin was sitting close to the door, holding the cereal box. And Camille, upon hearing Dan come in, toddled in to see him. With no diaper on and poop on her hand. "Hey, guys… where's Mommy?"

Sabine's voice roared from the living room: "Darling, I'm in here!" Dan was busy wrapping his head around what had happened here today as he rounded the corner of the living room to find flashing multicolored lights and a woman in a bright red feathered headdress. It was Sabine but not… "Honey, what's going on?" Sabine strutted in matching red stiletto heels, topless, and a rhinestone thong. "Here I am! The main attraction!" Dan set his briefcase down and scratched his head. "Sabine, what's happening? The kitchen is a mess… the kids are a mess… dinner isn't ready… Are you okay?"

She stopped strutting and turned to face him. Her eyes were not right. There was a tinge of something behind them. "Do you not appreciate having a star in your presence?" she bellowed. Dan was losing his patience, but there was a silence in the room and a clamminess to his hands that whispered: "Beware." "What's going on, Sabine?" She crossed over to him and sat him down. "You're just in time for the show!" she said. She disappeared into their bedroom and the music changed. Dan yelled over the music, "For the love of God, Sabine, what is happening?" She strutted out, runway style, with her arms stretched out almost like she really was on stage behind the couch. From behind the couch, she crouched and he couldn't see what she was doing until…

In an instant, the carpet behind her went up in flames. She retreated from there with a gas can in her hands, drenching everything in sight with gasoline. The flame caught to the outer recesses of the room. Dan stood and ran to grab Camille. He threw her into the kitchen. Sabine was so busy pouring the flammable liquid on everything that she didn't notice her headdress was on fire. "Sabine!" Dan yelled. "I know, darling, isn't it a fabulous show?" There was a wall of flames between them now and there was no getting her out. It sounded like she was singing. Dan knew he had minutes before everything would go up… minutes to save himself and the kids. He grabbed the kids and shoved them outside onto the steps. And in that moment, all of his memories of Sabine ran through his mind. The day they met, their first date, how beautiful she was the day they got married, and how wonderful it was to see her become the loving mother he knew her to be. He turned back, took a few steps in, and tried to approach the wall of flames. Heat licked at his face and the smoke was making him gag and cough. Could he get her? Could she be saved? He decided not and turned to leave. That's when he felt a searing pain on his left ankle. He looked down to see Sabine's burning hand had a hold of his ankle. He fell to the floor and tried to crawl towards the door. He glanced back and there was Sabine. Her head and body were engulfed in flames, her skin had been burned away, and now the only thing that was left were the muscles on her face and her glowing eyes. "My show… my show…" she muttered. He gave her one good hard kick on her hand and scampered to the door.

Chapter 4

It had been two hours of sheer chaos that burnt that house to the ground. The firetruck showed up, but it was too late. What was left of Sabine had been recovered and funeral arrangements were being made, and then the investigation began. The fire chief recalled not having seen a fire like this in decades. It had burned so hot that even parts of the steel frame of the house had melted. The detective walked the charred remains of what was once a happy home. Here was what was left of the kitchen, there were the remains of the living room, and in the bedroom everything had been destroyed… but in the corner of the closet… close to what would have been an outer wall of the house, situated under a pile of burnt roof tiles, laid what looked to be a book. The detective removed it from the rubble and dusted off the cover. It almost looked unscathed.

Hmm, she hadn't read a good book in a while… not since college. She cleaned it up a bit and shoved it into her purse. No one would miss this old book. As she walked to her car to type her final report she turned the title of the book over in her head. Was it a murder mystery? Was it about a serial killer? She was curious and couldn't wait until tonight to start reading *Next Victim*.

Flagler's Females

Blood. It was all over the pristine, white-lace-trimmed nightgown, soaking through to Mary's skin. How could such a little woman cough up so much blood? Ida had taken an oath with the Red Cross and had sworn to care for Mary. She wrung out the washcloth and wiped her face just as the next wave of coughing started again. Each cough shook Mary's frail body with such force that it rattled everything around her. More blood. It wouldn't be long now before 'consumption', as the doctor called it, would consume Mary Harkness Flagler.

Ida helped settle Mary back into her bed full of luxurious linens and fine goose-down pillows. Blood swirled around in the basin and mixed with the water as Ida washed it out. It was hard watching Mary suffer, and a reminder of how even wealth couldn't cure this… couldn't make her better.

Physicians of all kinds had been in and out of the house on Fifth Avenue and no one could help her. It was sad. How many times, on the days she had off from the Flaglers', had she met with her closest friend Lily and discussed the Flaglers? Henry was good to Mary. He provided everything she could ever want. It turned out that the only thing he wanted now was for Mary to get better, and even with all of his power and wealth he couldn't, for the life of him, make that happen.

Ida enjoyed taking care of Mary, although it was hard seeing her so sick. And she certainly wasn't fond of blood, but she found a new calling. And it wasn't just Mary she helped to take care of; it was Henry, too.

Yes, being fired from the circus was one of the best things to have happened to Ida. She knew she was too old to be a showgirl and when the ringmaster finally let the axe fall she wasn't surprised. Besides, so many wonderful things developed as a result of her employment with the circus: meeting Lily and Madame Fortuna had changed the course of her life. They had both taken a shining to the psychic and were fascinated with her tarot card readings. And, just like Madame Fortuna had predicted, Ida would leave the circus. "Not to worry," Fortuna told her when she rushed to seek her advice. "I see great things in your future, remember? The Sacred Feminine says to follow your heart, my dear."

And follow her heart she had, right to the office of the Red Cross. She needed a job and they needed help. Her first assignment was taking care of Mrs. Flagler. For the next two months 685 Fifth Avenue was her home, and things were certainly turning around.

—————

Several envelopes sat on the old table that Lily was using as a dresser/writing table. Each letter made itself clear: "Mary Lily Kenan, you get back here this instant before you damaged the family name." Yes, her mother definitely had a way with words. Lily paused for a second before she tore that letter into tiny pieces. *If I can just keep tearing*, she thought, *I can make it small enough where it never existed.*

Coming from an affluent family had its advantages, but she was having a hard time figuring out what those advantages were right now. She let out a heavy sigh and let herself fall back onto her single bed. Her pillow cradled her head and almost drowned out her noisy neighbors.

Her thoughts turned to Ida. She had really stumbled upon an ideal situation. Lily closed her eyes and thought if only she had a position like that… if only she had met someone with that kind of wealth it would change things… make things easier.

She pushed those thoughts away. She had been groomed by her mother to be pleasing to men… that was not the way. She would never allow herself to stoop so low. Just the thought made her feel dirty.

Besides, there were few men like Henry…kind, generous, and handsome. He was a lot of things that she found attractive. And if Lily were being honest with herself, she knew he felt something for her, too. She saw the flicker of desire in his eyes and could feel something radiating off of him when Ida was out of the room. She had allowed her mind to wander too far. Back to the situation at hand.

Returning to Kenansville, NC was not an option. It was so dull and monotonous, and now that she was in New York City she felt alive. No sir, that life was not for her. But, to be entirely honest, neither was this. She looked around at the one-room home she had shared with Ida before she started working with the Flaglers and the Red Cross. Mrs. Anderson's boarding house was certainly a far cry from the stately mansion she grew up in. Dingy rose-colored wallpaper dressed the room, and the ivory curtains that framed the only window were ivory at the top and then various shades of dirt led the floor.

Mary Lily or, as her friends would call her, Lily, stood and crossed the room. The day was turning into night and the light was fading. She lit two lamps, sat down at her desk, and prepared herself to write her dear mother back when there was a light persistent rapping at the door. She rose and cautiously opened it, only to find her best friend, Ida, standing there. Her face was flushed and her hair was a mess. She pushed past Lily and entered the room.

"Lil, she's dead," she whispered. Her eyes were wide and filled with a combination of sadness and surreal confusion. She was taller than Lily, so when she grabbed her by the shoulders and shook her Lily felt it. "She's really dead. I can't believe it."

Lily released herself from Ida's grasp and quickly closed the door. "We knew it was coming. Even Madame Fortuna told us it was coming, remember?" Ida sat on the edge of the bed, her head in her hands. Lily gently sat down right next to her and put a hand on her back. "Yes, I know. But now it's here and I guess I'm just shocked…"

She thought back to the night they went to see Madame Fortuna. She couldn't help but feel that the universe shifted at that moment. That there was a force bigger than her, bigger than the Flaglers at play here, and even though it was almost three months ago she remembered it well.

Two wide-eyed showgirls were lurking around Madame Fortuna's tent at the circus. They had heard the stories. Madame could see deep into people's futures. Everyone that had seen her had walked away with some insight into what the future held for them. Ida and Lily were curious for sure.

Just being here felt forbidden and ignited endorphins that flowed through their veins and made the hairs on the back of their necks stand up with excitement and anticipation. Light from inside her tent illuminated the ground outside like long arms gathering people and beckoning visitors to come in. The entrance was decorated with a long curtain of colorful beads in the middle, and adorning the exterior were scarves or long pieces of darkly hued colorful fabric that was foreign, exotic, looking like it was from a distant land.

Incense-perfumed air floated out and enticed the nostrils of each passerby. Yes, just walking by Madame Fortuna's tent attacked all of your senses, and if you weren't on guard or even the slightest bit open to her services you would find yourself seated next to her, listening intently to what was next for you. Ida and Lily were the latter of the two. The psychic world was fascinating, and they wanted to know what was in store for them.

Lily stepped into the edge of the light. Ida stood behind her, holding her hand, and curiously peered around Lily. A deep, melodic voice called out to the girls: "Mary Lily, Ida… I see you." Lily turned to Ida; both were wide-eyed, mouth agape as

Ida whispered in a hushed tone "… she knows our names…" Madame Fortuna continued, "Come in. Let me tell you your fortune." Her voice was intoxicating and irresistible. Lily squeezed Ida's hand as they moved through the beaded curtain.

There, in the middle of the tent, was a low round wooden table surrounded by large comfy pillows of all sizes. Lamplight created warmth and glow in the room. Oriental rugs covered the floor and large sheets with celestial figures on them adorned the inside walls. At present, the moon smiled and winked at Ida. She blushed.

And then, in the middle of all of these luxurious textiles, was Madame Fortuna. Her thick auburn hair was pulled back by a colorful scarf and cascaded down over the milky white skin of her shoulder. Her white off-the-shoulder blouse was pulled in by a soft brown fabric corset. Her legs were covered by a long deep purple skirt and she appeared to be sitting cross-legged, propped up on several pillows. Her eyes were closed. She sat erect with her long arms resting on her knees, palms up, the middle finger of each hand touching the corresponding thumb.

Lily approached. "How did you know my name?" Lily inquired. Without opening her eyes Madame Fortuna replied, "My dear, Madame Fortuna knows all. I have been waiting for you. The spirits have seen big things in store for you two." Ida mouthed, "They do?" Madame Fortuna's pose broke and she opened her eyes. She gazed upon her new visitors and gestured to the pillows on either side of her. "Come. Sit."

Her blue eyes were mesmerizing, and the girls felt as if they had been put under her spell. They did exactly as they were told and sat on either side of her. She pulled out a deck of cards from her skirt and sat them on the table in front of them. She closed her eyes again. "Give me your hands." Lily and Ida placed their hands in hers, closed their eyes, and were surprised to feel the energy flowing from Madame Fortune. They felt connected to her, as if she could tap into their very souls. All of their wants, desires, secrets were all hers now.

"Now, close your eyes and recite after me," Madame Fortuna instructed. "Sacred Feminine," she began, "… allow me to connect to your divine wisdom and knowledge." The girls repeated. "Please give me clear, direct messages." The air stirred around them. There was a definite presence in the room. "Please reveal to me what should be shown and how they may benefit from it."

Madame Fortuna released their hands and they opened their eyes. She placed both hands on the deck of cards, eyes still closed, and quietly chanted something over the cards. Then without looking she started shuffling the deck. "Ask me a question," she told the girls. Lily spoke up "Uh, what does the future hold for us?" Ida leaned over, nodding at Lily. "Oh yes. What does the future hold for us?"

Madame Fortuna pulled a card and put it in front of her. It was a hand cupping what looked to be a star. And then she selected two more cards and put them in front of each girl. Lily got a card that looked like a king in a chariot and Ida's was a craftsman hammering a star into metal.

She pulled one more card off of the deck and put it under the first card in the middle. There were three odd-looking stars and three people that appeared to be talking or following a list of instructions. Madame Fortuna inhaled deeply. "Ahh, yes. The first card states that opportunities are coming to you shortly. Ida, you will leave the circus and learn a new skill." Ida was lost in her thoughts and mumbled softly to herself, "A new skill…"

Madame Fortuna leaned over to Lily. "Now you, my dear, you are a driving force. Pay attention and don't take anything for granted." She pressed a finger to her lips in a hush. Lily stared back at Fortuna. Her eyes pierced her soul. There was a deeper meaning there. "Take advantage of *every* opportunity." Lily sat back and absorbed her words. Madame Fortuna continued, "The second middle card tells me that you two will have to work together to make this happen. Let me pull two more." Ida was barely paying attention, considering what new skill she would learn, but Lily was hanging on her every word.

"Cards, what will all of this hard work bring Lily and Ida?" The next card was unexpected. It was the Grim Reaper. The girls sucked in their breath and held it. Death? How could this be? "One more…" Fortuna sang. "Sometimes things are not always what they seem." The last card was a woman in a long flowing gown, holding a parrot, surrounded by nine funny-looking stars. Madame Fortuna sat back and seemed to relax a bit. "Yes… someone will die…" Ida gave out an audible gasp. "It's not either of you, but as a result you will fall into a luxurious lifestyle with great wealth." Lily and Ida stared at each other around Fortuna. They were at a loss for words. "That is all for now. Madame Fortuna has spoken. You must leave me." She pulled herself back into her beginning position —cross-legged, hands resting on her knees, middle finger touching her thumbs—and closed her eyes.

And just like that, it was over. The girls rose quickly and quietly and left the tent. Once outside, far from Madame Fortuna, they stopped, looked at each other, and embraced. Lily was the first to speak. "Oh Ida, did you hear her? We will live a luxurious lifestyle with great wealth." *And I'll be able to do it on my own*, she thought.

Her family was well known and wealthy already, but she wanted nothing to do with them. Ida backed away so she could see Lily's face. "But Lil, you heard her; someone is going to die." The concern in Ida's voice was noted. Lily smoothed Ida's hair. "My dear, you heard her: 'sometimes the cards are not what they seem'. I wouldn't focus on that."

She embraced her again. "I wonder what you are going to learn!" Lily was genuinely excited. Ida backed up and leaned against a wall. "Yes, but I'll be leaving the circus. You heard her say that. What will happen? Will I see you?" As excited as Lily was, Ida was nervous. Lily put her arm around her friend's shoulders. "You have nothing to worry about. She said this is something we'd be working on together. Remember? And we'll always be together."

———————

"You look good in black. It suits you." Lily was admiring her friend's reflection in the mirror. Ida spun around. "Lil, no one looks good in black." Lily shrugged. "Well, what else are you going to wear to a funeral? So, you'll wear it…" She stood, walked over to Ida and straightened her bonnet, and continued. "…and look fetching doing it!"

Ida swatted Lily's hand away. "Oh stop." But Ida knew she was right. Mr. Flagler, or rather Henry (he had asked her to call him that from now on) seemed to prefer her company when he was home. She realized her job now was to comfort him, tend to him, make sure he ate, drank, and slept. It had only been three days since Mary had passed, but it appeared that Ida would stay on to help care for Henry. He was kind and generous.

Lily was still a showgirl at the circus but it wasn't forever. And if everything went according to plan, Ida would be the new Mrs. Flagler in no time. Lily had been fortunate to be educated in feminine ways. How to be charming, intriguing… how to play the flirtatious girl if need be. It was expected for her to marry early, so she had been trained how to say things and when to say them. Lily taught Ida everything she knew with the intention that one day, it would work to her advantage. Ida had no experience with men. She had kissed a boy or two but nothing serious. Many nights they sat up, Lily whispering about men and what she knew to be true. In the end, it was all a mystery until each of them had their own experience.

Over the next few months, his grief seemed to lessen and he took a real interest in Ida. She remembered everything Lily had said and Henry responded most favorably. At first, it was to sit with him and then have dinner together. They would go out for strolls, and on one late summer evening Ida was surprised to find her hand in his as they gazed at the sun setting over the trees of Central Park.

The sky was streaked with various shades of pink, blue, and purple. Ida was admiring it when Henry brought her over to a bench and motioned for her to sit. She took her seat, still looking up at the sky. Ida thought she saw a large pink elephant made of clouds in the sky and turned to Henry to bring his attention to it, when she noticed he had dropped to one knee.

Surprise was the expression that Henry read on her face, but he proceeded nonetheless. He enveloped her hand in both of his and looked deep into her eyes. "Ida, I'm a man of few words, and I know this is fast, but…" He produced a small dark blue velvet ring box from his jacket and continued. "… will you do me the honor of becoming my wife?" He looked unsure of what she would say and her reaction, throwing her arms around his neck, was his answer. She embraced him, breathed him in and then pulled back, kissed him on the cheek, and offered her ring finger.

––––––––––

Lily was happy for Ida but she wasn't surprised. Madame Fortuna had predicted all of these events. Lily stared out the window of her room in deep thought while Ida lay on her bed, hand extended, admiring that shiny diamond on her finger. "Oh Lil, I'm so happy. Mrs. Henry Flagler!" She tried on the name for size. "Henry is a good man." She rolled over and looked at Lily. "And think of all the things we'll be able to do. I'll be able to get you out of here and into somewhere more fitting. We can travel." She sighed. "Lil, it's just like Fortuna said." Lily smiled in response to her friend's enthusiasm but continued to look out the window, deep in thought. "Yes," Lily answered. "It's just as she said…"

––––––––––

"I was wrong," Lily openly admitted with a ridiculous grin on her face. "White suits you." She threw her arms around her best friend in front of the mirror. "You are so radiant. I've never seen you happier." Ida's dress was the obvious white but was made of expensive French lace. She had never worn anything so extravagant. Ida broke their embrace to look at her friend's face. "Lil, I'm so happy you're my Maid of Honor. Henry was thinking about his cousin but he loves you, too. What more could a girl ask for?" She turned to look at Lily. "I can't believe this is happening," Ida said, letting out a nervous sigh. "Do you think we have time for…" her words trailed off. "Of course we do. I brought the board, silly." Lily beamed and almost tripped over herself to get the game out of her bag.

The Ouija board was the latest rage, and so much more telling than those silly cards Madame Fortuna had used. The girls cleared off Ida's side table. There was electricity in the air and everything became very still. Lily placed the planchette on the board and rested her delicate fingers on it. Ida did the same.

She was the first to speak. "Spirits, do I have your blessing on my marriage?" At first, the pointer seemed to hover… almost trying to decide where to go, and then it pointed to

"Yes". Lily went next. "Will they be together forever and ever?" It was a silly question and they both giggled like school girls. The planchette slid to the letters: "U-N-S-U-R-E." That put a damper on their playful happy mood. And then, without provocation, it spelled "B-E-T-R-A-Y-A-L".

They both let go of the pointer at the same time and looked at each other. "Lil, what does THAT mean?" A confused, hurt look washed over Ida's face. "I… I have no idea," Lily replied.

Lily quickly put the board back in the bag she'd brought it in. The two girls stood for a moment, not knowing what to say, and then Ida broke the silence: "It's just a stupid game."

After the wedding, Ida and Lily still saw each other. Their meetings were usually in Lily's room so they could talk and gossip without being seen. Ida confessed all of the details of her wedding night. Lily confided in Ida that the ringmaster was less than pleased with her. He said she was getting too old and brought in younger girls for her position up front. It concerned her, but Ida reassured her that everything would be fine and that she would always help her.

Then the day came when, again, there was a feverish, persistent knock on Lily's door. And just like last time in rushed Ida, a worrying blur of concern. "Oh my God, Lil, we're moving. He's making us move!" Ida burst into tears and hugged her friend. "What are we going to do?" Ida said through sobs.

Lily held her friend and, just like a warm blanket, she completely calmed the situation with her. "We'll do just as we always have done. It's going to be fine." Lily broke away and grabbed the Quija board from under her bed. She knew this would make Ida feel better. She set it on the bed and both girls sat down next to it. It only took a second for the planchette to start moving. They hadn't asked a question, but it appeared that something was trying to tell them something.

It spelled out "F-A-R-A-W-A-Y". Ida was the first to respond. "Yes, faraway… I'm moving far away." Her tear-stained face looked at Lil for a second before the pointer started moving again. "T-R-U-E-L-O-V-E". Ida broke the silence. "Well, I love Henry. So this must be the right choice. Right, Lil?" Lily looked at her and said, "Absolutely."

The Flaglers left New York a few months later. Things had been very busy, and packing took up most of Ida's time, but they were all able to get together for a few dinners before they left. Henry promised that he would send Ida to see Lily and that Lily was always welcome to join them in St. Augustine.

Ida had left Lily a substantial amount of money that would cover her rent for a while, and they wrote to each other almost every day. The letters would come in bundles, and Lily sat and read every single one. She missed her friend, and always looked forward to getting her letters.

As the months went on, the bundles were getting smaller and smaller. And the funds Ida had left were becoming less and less. Lily sent letters asking for more, but they went largely unanswered. She was starting to feel something she had never felt before—desperation. What were her options? She picked up a few side jobs, but things were very difficult.

The letters were now dwindling to one or two a week. Lily thought that she and Ida would always be friends. That they would always be together. Not having enough money didn't bother her—there were always ways to make a few extra cents —but it was Ida's silence that hurt. The spot in her heart where her love for Ida had been started to grow a festering, necrotic wound. It poisoned her thoughts and left a bad taste in her mouth. Why had Ida given up on their friendship? She was hurt beyond measure and needed an answer.

It was almost dinner time when Anna, Ida's maid, informed her that there was a woman at the door asking to speak to her. "She says her name is Lily." Ida was sitting at her dressing table, trying to decide on the right jewelry to wear, and the name startled her. Lily was here. And from some dusty corner came all of the old endearing feelings she had had for her friend.

Lily was here. She was really here. She finished up in the mirror, making sure that the fourth coat of red lipstick was in place… Yes, the board had said always four coats. Then she rose, descending the staircase in record time to see Mary Lily Kenan standing in the hall of her house.

Lily's gaze was averted upwards to the painted ceiling with gold leaf trim when she realized Ida was right there with her. Their eyes met, Lily dropped her bags, and the two friends embraced. "Lil, I can't believe you're here! It's so good to see you. You'll stay, won't you?" Lily hugged her old friend. "Yes, of course I'll stay, if that's all right with Henry!" she exclaimed. Ida was thrilled to have her old friend back. "It will be like old times!" Ida beamed. "Like old times… yes…" There was a sharpness in Lil's voice that Ida couldn't put her finger on, but no bother.

Over the next two weeks the friends did everything together. They went for long walks in the garden, went shopping, and even took Ida's yacht out with some of her friends. St. Augustine was full of lively parties and influential people. This was the oldest city in the country, and there was an abundance of things to do, but it was more than that. This city had a charm to it that tamed even the most reckless of businessmen. Was it the water? Maybe. Ponce de Leon certainly thought so. Lily loved everything about it.

The women also seemed to pick up right where they left off. Their late-night Ouija board meetings also resumed. Once things seemed good between them Lily pulled out the Ouija board. "For old time's sake?" Lily inquired. Ida squealed, clapping her hands. Now *there* was the girl Lily remembered. "Wait Lil, stay here." Ida ran out of the room and was back in a flash. "Let's use this one," Ida remarked as she started laying out her Ouija board.

Lily was taken back by the beauty of the board. It was one of the most elaborate she had ever seen. It was made of teak and trimmed in gold leaf, with jewels embedded in the board. Ida stared dreamily at it. There was an odd trance-like state about her now. Lily was speechless. It was beautiful.

Ida spoke then in a hushed, quiet tone: "This board has brought me to my one true love, Lil." Lily looked at her, confused. "But Henry is here, Ida. You love Henry," Lily said. Ida continued in that trance-like state, "Henry. Yes… but the board has been telling me things." Ida looked up at Lily then. "Lily, the Czar of Russia loves me. He wants us to be together."

Lily was thoroughly confused, but didn't let on. Instead, she listened to everything Ida had to say, and when they asked the board questions about the czar Ida was right. The board confirmed Ida's admission: the czar was in love with Ida. Lily couldn't believe how wonderfully convenient this was, and when they were finished Lily suggested, "You should send the czar something. To let him know that you're interested." Ida was still in her dream world when she responded with, "Oh my gosh, Lily, you're right! I know just the thing."

Over the next few weeks, the girls continued their whirlwind activities. They went for walks, they went shopping, took Ida's yacht out for a sail and Lily met all of Ida's friends. The dinners with the Flaglers were lavish and delicious. Henry was as charming as ever, and all of them seemed to pick up right where they left off.

———

A little after dinner every night Lily would retire to her room and write letters and read until it was her bedtime. It was late one night that she found she couldn't sleep. She donned her dressing robe and slippers and headed downstairs. Surely all she needed was some night air to settle her.

The moon was full. It bathed the veranda and the entire expanse of the lawn in moonlight. She emerged from the house, and was so focused on the beauty of the yard she hadn't noticed a figure sitting in a chair in a spot that the moonlight didn't touch. A voice came out of this dark spot: "Lily. What are you doing out here?" Lily jumped slightly and then recognized the voice right away.

"Oh! Henry, you startled me!" she whispered. "I couldn't sleep," she continued. "And the yard was so beautiful… I had to be a part of it." With that, Henry stood and quietly walked over to the pillar at the side of the steps of the veranda. She could just make out his face. The moonlight accentuated his mustache and highlighted every coarse hair. She crossed over and seated herself on the edge of the railing next to the pillar. He turned to face her. The shaft of light coming in behind her made her glimmer. Her luminosity overwhelmed him.

They were still a few feet apart, enough to be proper in public. He took a long drag off of the cigar he was smoking and then exhaled. "Lil, you shouldn't be out here by yourself. It's dangerous." The smoke billowed and curled around him. It floated over to her and she breathed it in. "Is it? Well, doesn't that sound fun," she said playfully. She moved closer, leaned in, and gestured for him to give her his cigar. He complied.

Henry watched, transfixed by what she was doing. He was bewildered by her brazen display of uncultured behavior. No lady would have ever done this. She raised the cigar to her lips and pulled in a long drag off of the cigar, then tilted her head back and blew out the smoke. Henry was mesmerized.

She continued, "It's been a while since I've seen you, Henry. I can't say you haven't crossed my mind." She hopped down off the railing and was within a foot of him. She took another long drag off of his cigar and handed it back to him. "Henry, I have to tell you something about Ida. I'm worried about her." She blew out the smoke and then locked eyes with him as she spoke.

Henry turned his body so he was facing her now. They were standing so close to each other, it wasn't proper. "What has you worried, Lil?" He stared at her face, studying her delicate features. Concentrating on her lips. He felt something stir. Lily continued. "Ida has been speaking of the Czar of Russia. The board is telling her things."

Henry knew all about this. It was a source of embarrassment for him. He turned his focus to the yard again, considering how to address this. "I know all about it. She bought him a ring a week ago and sent it to him. This nonsense has to stop." Lily felt bad. She touched his shoulder and said, "I'm so sorry you're going through this. But I'd like to think that everyone's true love is out there…" She placed her hand on top of his. "… I know mine is."

Their eyes met. Electricity coursed through Henry as she touched him. This woman pulled on him. It made him think things that weren't proper for a married man of his stature. There was her age to contend with as well. But she pulled on him… she always had. She dropped her hand and started to walk away. "I'll be performing a small concert tomorrow evening. I'd love it if you were there." She turned but kept her eyes on him, and said with as much breathlessness as she could muster "…goodnight…"

———————

The next night Ida and Henry took their seats in the front row in the square. It was an outdoor concert and Henry couldn't help but feel that there was something on the wind. It smelled of unrest and possibility. He wasn't sure if it was a good thing, but it had a hold of him either way. He sat still and watched Lily ascend the makeshift stage. Her pale cream lace dress hung on her and swayed as she sauntered. Henry dared not move for fear of giving away the stirring he felt for her.

Her performance was magnificent. She was an expert entertainer and a skilled vocalist. She was developing a local following, and it was obvious she could have her pick of any of these young suitors but her gaze—that heated gaze—always returned to Henry.

"Oh Lil!" Ida gushed. "You were spectacular!" She shoved flowers into her friend's arms. "You're too kind. It wasn't my best performance…" Lily offered up. Ida turned her head in Henry's direction and pulled on his sleeve. "Henry, tell Lil how amazing she was…I'm going to say hello to Mrs. Cartwright." And she was off.

Henry took a moment to form the words. He had to be careful. "Lily, your performance was top-notch," he said loud enough for everyone to hear, and then whispered under his breath just so she could hear him, "One might say… bewitching." He glanced at her to see if she caught what he said. She didn't say a word, but the comment registered in her eyes.

That night the wind picked up. You could hear the Spanish moss being blown around. It was similar to when a woman takes her hair down and shakes it out… it was a rustling of sorts. It was loud enough to wake Henry. He stepped out onto the veranda and gazed at the moonlit night. The yard was awash in a bright light that reminded him of the delicate pale skin of a woman's back.

It was nights like this that had made St. Augustine so appealing to him. It was a beautiful city, and he was intent on making it a destination with the railroad and hotels he was building. He crossed the veranda, a cigar in hand, and went to his usual spot where he sat at night. This was his thinking spot. What would be his next move? Other people were building in St. Augustine, and he had to figure out how to get to them.

And then there was Ida. What in the world was he going to do with her? He leaned back in his chair and rubbed his face. It was one thing when she wanted to do her craziness in the house. He loved her, and it didn't harm anyone, but now it was extending beyond the house… out to their friends… even his business partners seemed to notice she wasn't right.

He was mulling this thought over in his mind and was bringing the cigar to his mouth to light it when two hands rested on his shoulders from behind. It startled him and he turned around in defense. "Easy there, killer." Lily giggled. "I won't hurt you." Henry relaxed.

"Lil, thank goodness it's you. But again, you really shouldn't be out here." Her hand trailed across his shoulders. He inhaled sharply and wanted to push her away, but he couldn't. He wanted more. He took her hand in his and gently pulled her around in front of him. He sat closer on the edge of his chair and leaned his head into her body. Her dressing gown smelled of lavender and perfume, and just beyond that he detected something musky and female. Henry closed his eyes and relished the feel of her hands playing with his hair. In all the years, with all the women he had known, it had never been like this.

"Lil," he started. "I…I don't know what to do about Ida." He let out a breath. "She told Mrs. Cartwright about the czar tonight," Lily quietly confided. "No…" Henry shook his head. "No… please tell me she didn't," he said. Then in the doorway leading back into the house, they heard, "That's right. I told her." It was Ida.

She was wrapped unusually tight in her dressing gown. Her hair was a mess and she had red lipstick, the kind she insisted on applying six or seven times before they left the house, smeared across her tear-stained face. Lily backed away from Henry. "Look at you two. Isn't this lovely." Her voice sounded different, strange. She moved in closer. It was dark but there was an energy she was emitting. It was coming off of her in waves.

She stepped into a moonlit patch on the veranda. Henry saw the dilated insanity welling up in her eyes as she stared at them, and then a flash of something shiny and metallic. Before Henry had time to register what this object was in her hand she was upon Lily, slashing and desperately trying to make contact with any part of her. Lily fell back onto the wood floor and Ida was quick to pin her down. Lily's arms were pinned by Ida's knees as she straddled her. Lily was helpless.

Ida looked down at her as she struggled. "All these years…I thought you were my friend… "When Mary died 'Oh Ida, black is your color' no wait, when Henry and I married it was 'Oh Ida, white is really your color…'" Lily stopped struggling and just looked at Ida. She was in there but it wasn't her. If she could say the right thing she might be able to stop her. "Ida… We're friends… we always will be… and I meant everything I said!" she pleaded. Ida's nostrils flared. She inhaled deeply and closed her eyes.

"You know, Lil," she began. Her voice was shaky, almost like she was on the verge of laughing hysterically. "I never told you what color I think you look best in…" She got close to Lily's face and ran the flat part of the knife against her cheek. The feel of the cold steel terrified Lily. They were eye to eye when Ida whispered to her, "I think you'll look great in red. How about we stain that pretty dress?" She sat up fast as Lily started to scream. "HENRY! ANNA! OH DEAR GOD! SOMEONE HELP!" Lily yelled.

"You can scream all you want. I locked Anna in her room, and that cigar that Henry is so fond of has arsenic in it." She raised her arms above her head, holding the handle of the knife in both hands. That's when something flashed out of the corner of Lily's eye. Whatever it was struck her on the head and completely knocked her off of Lily.

Lily scrambled to her feet before Ida had a chance to get up. She looked around. Henry was standing in the moonlight, holding a large gardening shovel. His clothes were disheveled and his hair had fallen into his face. He looked at Lily, threw the shovel down, and pulled her into his arms. The strength of his embrace and the realization of what almost happened humbled Lily and she collapsed into him. The two melted to the floor and became a soft mass of coos and crying.

———————

"How is she?" Lily asked. Henry looked at her and weighed his answer. He responded with, "The doctor says she's stable, but has quite the headache." Henry let out an audible sigh and sat down in the nearest chair. The past twenty-four hours had been just awful, and exhilarating at the same time. He'd like to say he didn't see this coming, but he was prepared for it. Henry had a gift for being able to predict things in business and, as it turned out, also his marriage. Being a man of his stature afforded him certain luxuries. It came in handy to have doctors and people in the government in his pocket. These were people who owed him favors, and he planned on cashing in. What to do with Ida? He was already speaking to a doctor who had a private sanitarium in New York for wealthy clients. She would be put into his care and taken care of for the rest of her life. And then there was that messy marriage situation. He knew plenty of politicians, and surely they could help bend the rules a bit, especially if your wife was deemed 'legally insane', right? Just like taxes, there were ways around everything.

Henry was deep in thought when Lily broke the silence. "I'd like to see her… before she goes…" She knew his plans. "I'm not sure that's a good idea," Henry said. His eyes were shadowed with apprehension. "The last time she saw you…" Henry trailed off, his thoughts going back to watching Ida slash at Lily. Later seeing the huge gashes in her dressing gown that, if they had made contact, would have been fatal.

"Henry," Lily softened her voice, lowered her eyes, and touched his shoulder gently. "Ida and I have been friends a long time. We have a bond," she reassured him. "I realize that," Henry continued, "but that bond didn't stop her from trying to kill you." She came over, sat on his lap, and played with his hair. He melted. "Now Henry," she began, "the hospital is secure and you will be right by my side." She kissed his cheek and whispered in his ear, "Everything will be just fine." Henry backed his head up a little to get a better look at her. She noticed he was blushing slightly—the desired effect. "If you would like to say goodbye that's fine, but I won't leave you alone with her. Do you understand?" Lily threw her arms around him. "Oh yes! I understand. Thank you!"

The carriage ride to the hospital wasn't long, but Lily and Henry both sat in silence. They were nervous. Lily stared out the window, wondering how this meeting would go. It would determine her future.

They arrived and were greeted by Henry's acquaintance, Dr. Carlos San Rio. The lobby was pleasant, decorated in pastel colors. Various patients in wheelchairs were out and about. Each one had a blanket on their lap and a dull, medicated smile on their face. A few of them were drooling on themselves.

They didn't seem violent or crazy. It appeared to Lily that Dr. San Rio had everything under control.

They went through the doorway and into a hall. The atmosphere changed here. The warm, fuzzy feeling of the lobby had slipped into something else. Most of the patients' rooms' doors were open. She peered in to see the rooms were clean, tidy. They walked further down the hall. Was it Lily or was it getting darker? Further down the hall, all of the doors had small windows at eye height and were closed. Behind those doors, she heard the moans and wails of their patients, their prisoners…

This is where they would keep Ida. She thought back to all those lonely, desperate days and nights when she hadn't heard from her friend. Lily wrote and wrote but received no letters back towards the end. Ida had dismissed her and threw away her friendship. The thought of that made those old wounds ache. She took a deep breath and pushed past it.

They reached room 224. The doctor stopped them before they entered. "I have to warn you," the doctor whispered. "You are about to see Ida as you have never seen her before. Please understand that things will not always be like this for her. We have certain procedures in place to keep her and everyone else safe." Henry and Lily looked at each other and nodded. Dr. San Rio unlocked the door and walked in. They followed behind him. The room was stark white with no windows. Lily looked past the doctor to see that the only furniture in the room was a bed and Ida was tied down to it. Henry's hand came up to his mouth to muffle an audible gasp. He pulled her head into him. "Lil, you don't have to see this," he said. "Henry, I'm okay. I have to do this. I have to see her," Lily stated as she released herself from his embrace.

Henry turned to the doctor to discuss his wife's treatment plan. Henry seemed distressed to see Ida in this state. Lily moved toward the bed. She was standing right next to her friend now. She gently touched her arm, moving her fingers over the restraint. Ida's eyes popped open. They immediately fell on her.

"Lily?" she said. Lily looked at her friend. "I'm here." She placed Ida's in hers. Ida's hand was so cold. Her voice was soft, barely a whisper, but Lily could hear everything she was saying. "You and Henry…" Ida trailed off. Her brow was a bit furrowed. She seemed confused. Lily looked down at her friend and squeezed her hand. "Don't worry, Ida," she said, and then leaned down near her ear. "…I'll take good care of him." Lily pulled back, made direct eye contact with Ida, and gave her a devious smile. "And this place will take good care of you."

The confusion on Ida's face lifted and a dark shadow replaced it. This was the Ida that Lily had seen the other night. Lily could feel Ida squeezing her hand. The sharpness of her nails gave Lil a start. "Oh, dear…" Lily said loud enough for Henry and the doctor to hear right before the screaming started.

"RED! RED! YOU'LL LOOK GOOD IN RED!!" Ida wailed over and over.

In a matter of seconds a group of people were on her, soothing her, injecting her with something that calmed her. Henry and Lily had been pushed aside, but were privy to the whole situation. It was a fast and furious rush of people pulling, moving, hushing, and soothing. Henry held Lily close and pressed her head into his chest. She smiled again, knowing that Ida's fate had been sealed. It had all been so easy.

Just as the ride in had been a silent one, so was the ride home. The new couple held hands as best they could. White gauze wrapped Lily's hand, but a few specks of fresh blood peeked through. Underneath it were the gouge marks from Ida. Occasionally, Henry's finger would run over her bandage. There was a heaviness to his thoughts but also a sense of relief.

Lily stared out the window. Her plan had all come to fruition. Just a few more minor details and everything would be in place. When they finally returned home Lily went straight to the room she had been staying in. She wasn't sure what the proper thing to do now was—should she stay in her room or attempt at staying in Henry's?

She was lost in thought when she closed the door to the room. She crossed over to the bed and there, sitting right in the middle of the bed, almost as if it were waiting for her, was Ida's Ouija board. How did it… where did this… She stumbled back a bit, surprised. She regained her composure and walked sensibly back to the bed. *Silly old game*, she thought. She was getting ready to toss it in the trash when she decided it would be fun to see what it had to say now, now that Ida wasn't in control of what it said. Lily put her fingers on the planchet and closed her eyes.

It immediately started moving. G-O-O-D. J-O-B. Lily let the message register. She was intrigued now to see what else it had to say. She had one very specific question to ask: "What color do I look good in?" Again, the guide moved on its own. She could feel something coursing through her now.

R was the first letter. She closed her eyes and surrendered to this feeling. E was the second letter. A color was starting to form… the last letter was D. RED. That word, this feeling coursing through her veins, was making her think strange thoughts. She shook her head and left the room to find Henry.

———————

As usual, during the day he could be found in his office. Sometimes a newspaper in hand, sometimes reading one of the many books he owned in his extensive library. Lily walked in and found him at his desk, writing a letter. "Hello, darling…" she breathed. She traced a finger on his desk around to where he was sitting. He was in the middle of writing and didn't look up until he was finished. "There," he said, adding his signature with a flourish. "Lil, be a dear and put this in the mailbox for me." He didn't even look up at her. He just handed the letter to her.

Lily took the letter and walked out. Once outside she turned the letter over in her hands. It was addressed to M.F., P.O. Box

128, New York, NY. It barely had time to be sealed. Lily peeled open the envelope and pulled the ivory-colored paper from it. The letter started the same as every other letter:

Dear Madame,

Greetings and salutations. It is my hope that this letter finds you well.

I write to you today to thank you for your assistance. It appears that after our meeting those things that you spoke of have come to pass. No doubt your help, as well as that of my maid, Anna, nudged the girls in the right direction.

Also, thank you for incorporating that Ouija board. It was like adding gasoline to a small fire. Things ignited and went up in flames rather quickly.

You'll be happy to know that one situation has already taken care of itself. Ida is now in the care of Dr. San Rio.

The other one, well let's just say that Anna has put the wheels in motion and I can already sense a shift. It's just a matter of time before THAT takes care of itself. I might help it

along a bit… accidents do happen, you know.

I have transferred the appropriate funds to your account.
Please do keep in touch.

Sincerely,

Henry M. Flagler

Lily stood on the veranda, completely shocked. Henry…
this whole thing had been planned? She shoved the letter back
into the envelope and looked around. Her heart was pounding
in her ears. It was the only thing she could hear. She tucked the
letter into the waist of her skirt. M.F. it could only be one
person… they were in on this together! Lily held her breath
and closed her eyes.

Rage coursed through her veins, and when she opened them
she only saw one thing. It was the color red and her gaze fell

on the garden shovel. It was time that Henry understood that everyone looks good in red. Especially when it's their own blood. She grabbed the shovel and made her way to the door. Before she even crossed the threshold of the house she called out, almost sing-song like, "Oh Henry?"

Bayou Balance

Tyler's boat flew over the water. The wind whipped at his hair and bugs battered his tan skin. It was just past sunset and the clouds were rolling in. He knew his time was limited. No one wanted to be out here at night… especially in the bayous of Louisiana.

The fish and gators sensed his apprehension. They usually glided out of the way, but they jumped… they couldn't get out of his way fast enough tonight. He was going where he shouldn't be going…to do something he knew he shouldn't be doing. He had tried everything, but there were only two things left. Both solutions were desperate, but one was not an option. At least not when you had a family.

He slowed down and turned into a worn boat path that lead deep into the swamp. The tall trees were draped with long strands of Spanish moss. The crickets were chirping. This environment felt distinctly female. It was almost as if they were the sentinels for the High Priestess.

Bianca was legendary. She grew up in a family that was proud to have voodoo passed down from generation to generation. Things were different now and somehow, somewhere along the road, voodoo had been given a darker undertone. It made her question its purpose. She knew with each interaction, every time she performed a ritual, she had the choice of using it for good or evil. Life had dealt her a heavy hand of cards, and that helped solidify the fact that she was capable of both. But it's all about perspective, isn't it?

She sat on the dock with a Voodoo Lady Cosmopolitan in her hand, waiting for the man she knew was coming. The spirits spoke to her last night and told her of his visit. She didn't know who he was or what he needed, but she could feel his desperation.

She took another sip just as she heard the buzz of an outboard motor coming up the channel. Stillness overtook her as she saw the boat slow down as it rounded the corner. A gentleman, maybe in his thirties, was captaining this vessel. His sandy blond hair was windblown, and accentuated his deeply tanned skin.

He disembarked and cautiously approached the woman in the chair. "Hello. My name is Tyler." He was wringing his hands and his brow was furrowed. She looked him up and down without moving. "Yes, I've been expecting you," she said in a deep, melodic tone. She rose upon her statement and started walking towards the house. Her skirt created a *shh-shh* sound as she walked, like she was hushing a baby.

Tyler relaxed a little and followed suit. They moved off of the dock and into the night. It was already so dark, but it seemed to Tyler that the further they moved in the darker it got. Soft, padded footsteps could be heard in front of him and the glass beads that adorned her long locks were knocking together to the rhythm of her step.

Just ahead, in the distance, was the pleasant glow of a house. Tyler breathed a sigh of relief. *Oh thank God*, he thought. Any escape from this swampy darkness that threatened to envelop him was surely a godsend.

The two entered the house and were in the kitchen. It was warm and cozy. Dried flowers hung from the ceiling. Something that smelled delicious was bubbling on the stove. Bianca instructed him to have a seat at the kitchen table while she lit a purple candle. "So, Tyler, what brings you here?" She was making conversation while she gathered the pieces for the ritual. "Well, I'm afraid I need your help." He trailed off but continued, "I was seeing this woman…" Instantly he regretted even talking about it. "But aren't you married?" Bianca inquired. "Y- Yes. How did—"

"The spirits know all," she sang as she picked up the bones, bowl, a lighter, a knife, and a few assorted colored candles. She sat down across from him and spread the candles out in front of him.

"Tyler, I want you to think about your intentions. What is it that you would like me to do?" His face was bathed in the warm glow of the candles, but there were shadows. He was not what he seemed. "I… I just want her to go away. I don't want her anymore, and she poses a real threat to my way of life."

Bianca took his hands in hers and closed her eyes. She instructed him to do the same. "I want you to picture the best-case scenario. Again, what is it that you want?" There was an energy building in the little room, but Bianca couldn't tell if it was good. And then a picture appeared in her mind. The poor woman…

She opened her eyes, released his hands. "You…" She searched his face for signs of empathy, remorse for what had transpired. There was none. Tyler looked at her and said, "I just want this taken care of…"

There was a moment of silence and then Bianca calmly said, "I understand. I'll take care of it." He seemed to relax a bit after that. She gave him two bay leaves. On one he wrote his name. On the other he wrote the woman's name. Then she spread out several candles—all different colors—and asked him to choose one. He reached for the red one. "Not that one," she said. Instead, he picked blue. She chuckled to herself. Naturally he would want protection, and a ritual done with a blue candle would ensure that. She lit the blue candle, blew out the purple one, and then lit the one she had picked out for him —the black candle.

She closed her eyes again, humming slightly, and rolled the bones. She was in the middle of reading them when he said, "What does it say?" Bianca smiled. "It's complicated but it looks like everything is aligning. Now, I just need a few things from you." He stammered a bit. "From m-me? Like what?" Bianca held up the knife. It glimmered in the light, all too happy to be of service. "I need a lock of your hair and a small amount of blood. You know, if you want to make this all go away." The expression on his face was one of shock. "Why do we… wait… this doesn't sound right."

Bianca stood up. "We don't have to do this." She smiled warmly at him. "You can see yourself out." She turned. "No, no… it's fine. I just wasn't expecting this…". She walked over, knife in hand, pulled up a good piece, and sliced right through it. "There. That wasn't so bad, was it?" The tone of her voice was like artificial honey—sugary sweet and too good to be true. She dropped the hair into the bowl. Then she picked up his left hand, examined it until she found his ring finger, and with the point pierced the tip. Tyler let out a soft muffled "Ouch!" She squeezed and squeezed until there was a steady stream. Her eyes lit up watching him squirm seated at the table.

A smile spread across her lips that Tyler wasn't entirely sure was good. She mixed the blood and hair and dropped it into a glass jar. She was chanting something when she lit the bay leaf with his name on it and dropped it in as well.

Immediately the room started to spin and everything was getting smaller. The walls were closing in on him and then he realized the walls were made of glass. He looked up just in time to see Bianca putting the lid on the jar. He was trapped inside the jar! Panic overtook him and he started screaming.

Next, she took the bay leaf with the woman's name on it. Sophia. Poor Sophia. She closed her eyes while she chanted and crushed the bay leaf. When she finished she blew the bay leaf into the blue candle, ensuring her protection from further damage. She would be protected and free. A brisk wind moved through the house, and some of the candle smoke and bay leaf was carried out on the night breeze.

Bianca turned her attention to the jar. This… this thing in the jar… needed to be dealt with as well. She picked up the black candle and tilted the jar. The flame danced around the glass. She took pleasure in watching the thing in the jar dance and jump to get away from the heat. Ha-ha… "Okay, Bianca," she said to herself. "Stop toying with him."

It was always good to maintain that balance—good vs evil—and so long as the good won the majority of the time Bianca was fine with those brief interludes with darkness. The black candle had a fair amount of wax built up. She poured the wax onto the top of the jar. It spread and oozed down the sides. Now it was sealed for good and it would be put away where all her nasty bits were. A dark corner that would be forgotten about… like Tyler had wanted for Sophia.

Bianca cleaned up, took her cocktail outside, and went back to the dock. It had been a productive night. She would have to thank the spirits later. I mean, how often is it that you can rid the world of darkness AND become the owner of boat?

Long Live the Queen

The inky black sky felt like an abyss. Angela stared out the side door of the CMC's helicopter and considered a few things. First, she considered her mission. There had been other side jobs over the years, but her main objective since she joined the Centralized Mission Command had been this assignment. Did she have her own agenda? Yes. Evil had to be stopped at all costs.

The second thing she was considering was her partner. The fact that she could hear him chewing and smacking his gum in their headsets over the whirl of the helicopter was, in a word, distracting. How could someone so brilliant be so annoying? Her thoughts wandered to all facets of her partner, Isaiah.

He was her partner in so many ways. "Hey," Isaiah broke the silence. "You okay over there?" The question crackled over her headset. "I… I dunno if I'm emotionally ready for this." She looked down and then glanced at him sideways. "We've been training for this." There were things she just couldn't tell him. "Yes, you're right," she offered up, knowing that this would probably be their last mission. She'd miss him.

Another crackly transmission over the headset came in from the pilot. "I hate to break up the party back there but it's almost go time." Angela looked out the side door and spotted her target. "Go in 5, 4…" She looked at Isaiah. There were no words. "3, 2…" She looked up at him one last time and locked it into her memory. "1."

Angela was first to jump. She could feel the cool night air racing over her face. She waited a few seconds and pulled the cord. It was a hard landing on top of the palace, but they nailed it. They cut the parachute cords, armed themselves with their weapons, and accessed the rooftop entrance. Angela was headed to the queen's quarters. Interestingly enough, there was no security, no guards.

They found her sitting in the reading room, reading a book. "Hello, Angela," the queen said, barely looking up. "Hello, Grandmother." Angela continued, "I'm sorry it had to be like this." Angela could hear Isaiah in her headset, turning over the newfound information. "…this is your grandmother?" Angela held her gun steady. Isaiah continued, "Wait. We're here for the file. Right?" she replied, "Change of plans, Isaiah."

The queen continued, "… I'm sorry, too." She dropped her book that had hidden two guns and fired off two shots without hesitation. Angela and Isaiah fell to the floor. The queen walked over to them quietly and said, "And that's why I'm the queen." She laughed a little, looking at the two of them. "You have to be one step ahead, my dear." She turned to leave. BANG! Angela watched as her grandmother fell to the ground.

She turned her head to Isaiah. "What grandmother does that to their grandchild?" Isaiah gasped. Angela whispered, "…thank you…"

The dark void was closing in, but it was all right. Her mission was complete.

A letter from the author…

Where does a story idea come from? That's a good question. I'm not sure I can come up with a general answer for that. But…for this anthology, I can think of two separate conversations I had with the two people that have the most influence over me (besides my kids).

The first conversation was short and went something like this:

"There's a GOTHIC ASYLUM at the next exit? Get over in the next lane. We have to check this out." My sister, Krista, graciously pulled off the highway and we had a lovely visit at the Trans-Allegheny Lunatic Asylum.

One thing that shocked me was the number of women back in the late 1800s who had been admitted with questionable diagnoses. Bad whisky, bad habits and political excitement, tobacco and masturbation, and my personal favorite - imaginary female trouble. We had a hard time accepting that this was some women's fate back then.

The second conversation was with my best friend, Tarin. "Did you know that Henry Flagler had three wives? The first died, the second was committed to a sanatorium and the third was much younger than him. Sounds suspicious…juicy… doesn't it?"

Growing up in Palm Beach County we visited White Hall, Henry Flagler's winter home almost every year we were in school. He was loved. He is still loved. But, he was a wealthy man, and back then, that excused a lot.

It was important to me that you understood that Flagler's Females, along with all of the other short stories here, are works of fiction. I did a lot of research on Henry and all of his wives as well as St. Augustine to get a feel for them as people and also to try and read between the lines. It is in no way meant to be a factual account of what happened.

This is fiction and my hope is that you enjoyed these tales of madness, maybe got a little creeped out, or thought something my best friend said "Where do you come up with this stuff?" If you think any of those things, then I feel that I have done my job.

Thank you for taking this journey with me.